Gopher to the Rescue!
A Volcano Recovery Story

by Terry Catasús Jennings
illustrated by Laurie O'Keefe

Something is different on the mountain.
Snowshoe hare hears the rumble from miles away.
Black bear feels the ground shake beneath her paws.

Gopher feels the earth move in his burrow.

Steam and ash burst from the top of the mountain. It looks like smoke.

Elk has never seen this before.

Squirrel sees black smudges on the snowy mountain.

The rumblings go on for days. The mountain is changing. A volcano is waking up.

But gopher just digs and digs in his burrow.

Early one morning, the animals feel rumbling and trembling and shaking more terrible than they've ever felt before. They hear a terrible sound.

The top of the mountain slides away. Snow and rock slide down the mountain and into the valley. Then, the mountain explodes!

The blast from the explosion blows down all the trees. The top of the mountain disappears in a cloud of ash and rock. The volcano is erupting!

The animals try to run away.

The heat, ash, or the force of the explosion kills many animals. But gopher is safe in his burrow, with plenty of tasty roots and bulbs to eat.

When the shaking stops and the roar quiets, gopher begins to dig again. He digs through soil and then he digs through gritty warm ash, sand, and pebbles. He wonders, *Where did all this stuff come from?*

When he reaches the surface, blown-down trees cover the landscape like toothpicks. The world is gray and dry and hot.

Gopher is not alone.

Ant and beetle crawl around on the crust formed by the hot, dry ash. They find plenty of food in the dead wood and plenty of places to hide.

From his home under a rotten log, mouse sticks out his nose. He's confused. But the tree is still home and he has tasty bugs to eat.

Even though his world has changed, gopher digs and digs. He mixes the soil from his tunnels with the crusty ash, adding life-giving nutrients. The nutrients help plants to grow. Gopher helps the mountain recover.

Salamander and toad pollywogs survive the blast under the ice and in the mud at the bottom of a lake. Come summer, when it's time for them to live their adult life on dry land, they find the world dry and hot. They use gopher's tunnels to find shade and get around in the hot, dry landscape. They head to the cool, damp forest nearby or to new ponds created in the blast area.

Insects return to the mountain right away, flying in on the wind. Spiders float in on silken threads. Seeds blow in from near and far.

Days turn into weeks and weeks turn into months. Some seeds take root on top of gopher's tunnels and grow into plants.

Birds also visit the mountain right away and eat tasty bugs and seeds. They perch on small islands of plants and flowers that survived the blast.

Weeks pass and months pass. But there are no places to nest. Birds can't live on the mountain, not yet.

Elk often explores the mountain. At first, he finds young trees that survived the blast under the snow. As months turn into years, saplings sprout from seeds. They're a little snack, but they're not enough for him. He needs to take cover in the shady forests nearby—the forests that were not damaged by the heat, or the rocks, or buried under the ash. He'll return to live on the mountain when there's plenty of food to eat and plenty of places to rest and hide.

Months and years pass. Slowly hemlocks, firs, fireweed, and lupine grow. Animals visit. When they find enough food and shelter, they can stay on the mountain.

Gopher still digs and digs, looking for new roots and bulbs to eat—making the ground fertile for more seeds to grow.

Years have turned into decades. Trees and bushes dot the landscape. Elk, squirrels, snowshoe hares, and black bears are returning to the fertile, new habitat on the mountain.

Some areas may never be as they were before the big blast. But of one thing we can be sure— gopher will still dig and dig . . . and the mountain will continue to change.

For Creative Minds

What and Where Are Volcanoes?

A volcano is a vent in the Earth's surface where magma, gases, and ash erupt. It also refers to the landform constructed by erupted material. Erupting lava builds new land but volcanic explosions can destroy the area around them.

Volcanoes are active (erupting or expected to erupt in the near future), dormant (like sleeping), or extinct (not expected to erupt again).

To understand volcanoes, we have to understand a little bit about the Earth. The Earth is made up of four layers. It might help to imagine the Earth as a kiwi fruit.

The outer layer is the Earth's *crust* (represented by the kiwi's skin). It is very thin compared to everything else. If you could dig very deep, you could dig through the crust. But nobody can dig that deep—not even oil drillers or miners.

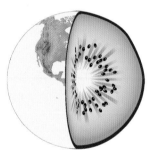

The next layer is the Earth's *mantle* (represented by the kiwi's green flesh). It is a dense, hot layer of semi-solid rock.

The Earth's two inner layers (called the *core*) are mostly iron and nickel. The *inner core* (represented by the white center of the fruit) is solid. The *outer core* (represented by the black seeds) is in between liquid and solid—more like an oatmeal mush (molten).

The crust is only 5 to 25 miles (8 to 40 km) thick.

The mantle is about 1800 miles (2900 km) thick.

The inner core is 770 miles (1250 km) thick.

The outer core is 1400 miles (2200 km) thick.

TECTONIC PLATES

The Earth's crust and the top part of the mantle are broken into puzzle-like pieces called *tectonic plates*. These plates glide past, pull away from, or move toward each other.

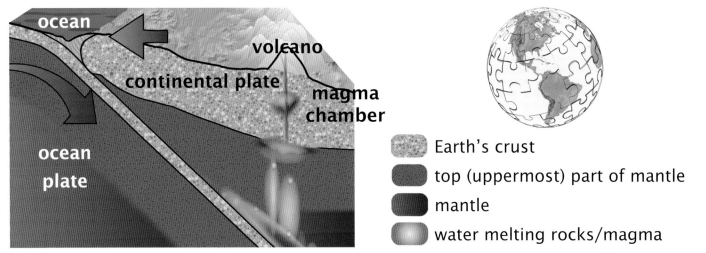

Earth's crust

top (uppermost) part of mantle

mantle

water melting rocks/magma

As the cooler and denser ocean plate sinks into the warmer mantle of the continental plate above, temperatures are hot enough to drive water out of the plate.

The water causes part of the mantle to melt—making *magma*. Since magma is less dense than the rock around it, it moves up—just as a balloon floats up into the air.

As it moves up, it melts the solid rock in the Earth's crust along the way.

The magma pools as a *magma chamber*. Gases in the magma can cause it to erupt, sometimes explosively!

The red lines show where the plates meet. What do you notice about the location of most volcanoes (shown in circles) and the location of the plates?

There are some areas that are not along plate boundaries where magma erupts at the Earth's surface. These places are called *hotspots*. As the plate moves over the hotspot, a chain of volcanoes sometimes forms, such as the Hawaiian Islands.

Volcanoes also form where two plates pull apart. These volcanoes may make mountain ranges and are called rift volcanoes.

Once magma reaches the Earth's surface, it's called *lava.*

Most of the world's volcanoes are along plate boundaries, like the boundary around the Pacific Ocean. This area is known as the Ring of Fire.

Natural Disasters and Habitat Changes

Living things rely on the living and non-living things in their habitat to meet their basic needs. Changes in their habitat can affect how their needs are met. Volcanoes, hurricanes, earthquakes, tsunamis, floods, tornadoes, and wildfires are just some of the natural disasters that can change a habitat in a very short time.

Scientists can sometimes warn humans that a natural disaster is coming, but wild animals have to rely on their own senses. Some living things may survive, but not all. How does life return to an area that has been destroyed?

Mount St. Helens in Washington State erupted on May 18, 1980, destroying habitat. Based on past volcanic eruptions, scientists knew that the area around the volcano would eventually recover. They spent years observing and documenting how the area recovered. This information helps us to understand how life returns to any area that has been totally changed or destroyed.

Which came first? Can you put the events in order of how they happened to unscramble the word?

D Once there were enough plants for food and shelter, animals moved in. Eventually meat-eating animals (predators) came back to eat the plant-eating animals (prey).

B The volcano erupted. The force of the explosion blew down trees. Rock and ash covered the land, making it hard for plants to grow.

L Seeds start new plants. Wind carried in seeds from surrounding areas. Visiting animals dropped seeds that were stuck in their fur or deposited when they went to the bathroom. The seeds that fell to the ground either grew into plants or became food for other animals.

I Plants provide food and shelter for animals, but they need water and nutrients to grow. As gopher dug, he softened the ground and mixed the buried soil from his tunnels with the ash, making it easier for plants to grow. Animals visited looking for food to eat. As these animals walked around, they helped break up the ash to uncover the soil.

U A few living things survived the blast. Some young trees and bushes survived buried under snow. Some animals survived in underground burrows—as long as they had food to eat. Some rodents and insects survived in rotten logs. Hibernating frogs, toads, and salamanders survived under the lake's ice.

Hands On: Pressure and Melting

Imagine the weight or pressure of a million rocks sitting on top of you! The deeper into the Earth, the more rocks there are so the more pressure there is. Pressure deep in the magma makes gases (like water vapor and carbon dioxide) dissolve. As the magma rises and pressure decreases, the gasses make bubbles—like those in a can of soda.

What happens when you shake a can or bottle of soda and then open it? *Do this outside and point the soda away from you or other people when you open it.*

When the soda is being made, carbon dioxide (a type of gas) is added with the soda flavor. This gas is what makes the bubbles in the soda you drink. As the can sits, the gas tries to escape from the soda and a small amount

usually rises to the top of the can. That's what makes the small popping sound when you open a can. Shaking the can adds energy. That energy separates the gas from the soda water—making tiny bubbles in the liquid. The bubbles increase the pressure inside the can and will explode out of the high-pressure environment into the lower pressure atmosphere as soon as you open the can.

Bubbles of water vapor and other gases in the magma react almost the same way as the soda bubbles. As the gas bubbles push the magma towards the surface, they can expand up to thousands of times their original volume—the eruption!

How can a solid melt into a liquid? Heat. The amount of heat needed and the length of time depends on the solid to be melted.

Place some ice cubes in a microwave-safe bowl. Heat the bowl of ice for 15 seconds. Open the door and look for evidence of melting. If you do not see evidence of melting, heat it for another 15 seconds. Repeat until you see evidence of melting, then stop. Record the time required to show some melting. Now, follow the same procedure with 2 oz. (1/4 cup) of chocolate chips. Did both substances have equal melting times?

Water boils at 212°F (100°C). The temperature needed to melt rock depends on the type of rock but ranges from 1300°F to 2400°F (700°C to 1300°C). Do you think that your microwave could heat a rock until it melts? Why or why not?

Go to the book's homepage at www.SylvanDellPublishing.com for more free activities including time-elapsed sequencing using actual photos of the Mount St. Helen's recovery, changing environments, information on how scientists monitor volcanoes, how volcanoes behave, and different types of volcanoes.

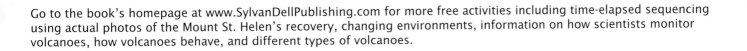

Thanks to Peter Frenzen, Mount St. Helens Monument Scientist, US Forest Service; Frederick J. Swanson, Research Geologist with the USDA Forest Service, Pacific Northwest Research Station and co-editor of *In the Blast Zone: Catastrophe and Renewal on Mount St. Helens* and *Ecological Responses to the 1980 Eruption of Mount St. Helens*; and to Liz Westby, Outreach Assistant and Carolyn Driedger, Hydrologist/Outreach Coordinator at the USGS Cascades Volcano Observatory, for reviewing this book for accuracy.

Library of Congress Cataloging-in-Publication Data
Jennings, Terry Catasús.
Gopher to the rescue : a volcano recovery story / by Terry Catasús Jennings ; illustrated by Laurie O'Keefe.
p. cm.
Summary: When a volcano erupts, Gopher is among the few animals to survive but the tunnels that he digs once the earth stops shaking helps the mountain recover by providing shade and soft soil for animals and plants to make a fresh start. Includes facts and activities.
ISBN 978-1-60718-131-6 (hardcover) -- ISBN 978-1-60718-141-5 (pbk.) -- ISBN 978-1-60718-151-4 (english ebook) -- ISBN 978-1-60718-161-3 (spanish ebook) 1. Pocket gophers--Juvenile fiction. 2. Saint Helens, Mount (Wash.)--Eruption, 1980--Juvenile fiction. [1. Gophers--Fiction. 2. Saint Helens, Mount (Wash.)--Eruption, 1980--Fiction. 3. Volcanoes--Fiction.] I. O'Keefe, Laurie, ill. II. Title.
PZ10.3.J4295Gop 2012
[E]--dc23
2011034325

Also available as eBooks featuring auto-flip, auto-read, 3D-page-curling, and selectable English and Spanish text and audio
Interest level: 004-009 Grade level: P-4   Lexile® Level: 740L Lexile® Code: AD
Curriculum keywords: basic needs, change environment, change over time, earth processes (fast/slow), earth properties: rocks, water, soil, atmosphere; habitat, inquiry, interconnectedness, landforms, map, natural disasters, plate tectonics, sequence

Manufactured in China, December, 2011
This product conforms to CPSIA 2008
First Printing
Published by Sylvan Dell Publishing
Mt. Pleasant, SC 29464